MEET SARA . . . AND HER SPOOKY FRIENDS!

After class, Jake slowly walks to Sara's house.
How did I get into this?
BANG! BANG!
Inside the house:
Hi! I am Mr. Bones. Come on in!
How do you do?
Eeeek!

Jake, are you okay?
No! Spooky . . . ghost!
Hi!
Oh! Do not worry. Ghosty is my buddy!
We will show you the house now.
Look out!!!
Oh! Do you want to pet Miss Spider?
No, thank you!

Time to work.
Where should we start?
Far away from this place!
Bug juice, anyone?
Uh. No . . . thank you.
Where did that come from?

Hey!
Over there!
That is so nice of you to greet Wolfy! He is very shy, you know.
He wants to play ball.
Uh, here . . . catch.
POP!

We lose a lot of balls that way.
What else could be in this house?
He wants to see more . . .
. . . and we have much more!

Look, Jake! Here . . .
. . . and here . . .
. . . and here!
I have got to get out of here . . . now!
Jake makes for the door.
What about the project?

We can finish the project later . . . on the phone!
Did you hear that? He is going to call me!

I really think he liked us.
Oh, yes! He LOVED us!

SPOOKY COOKOUT

People stare at Sara and her friends . . .
. . . instead of watching where they are going!
CRASH!
There are a lot of bad drivers out today.

Sara and her friends are here!
Gulp.
What ARE they?
Spooky!
Mr. Bones tries to help.
I hope you like your burgers well done.
Oh, dear!
I added a little something for flavor.
Mmmm. Crunchy.
Oh? What did you add?
Bugs! Tasty bugs!
I am going to be sick.

Later, Wolfy shows off.
I am NOT getting in the pool after this!
Ya-hoo!
Ghosty tries to show off, too.
Watch this!
Mommy!
Eeek!
Cool!
The family is scared.
Waaaa!

Ghosty tries one more time.
Want to see a magic trick?
Probably not!
Yes!
Spell, spell, spell so cool . . .
. . . do it now —empty this pool!
POOF!
The pool is still full . . . full of SNAKES!
Aaahhh!
Run for your life!
Hmm. That is not what I wanted.
Spell, spell so NOT cool . . .
. . . do it now— UN-fill the pool!
Help! Help!

Well . . . the pool is not full anymore.
Help!
RATTLE
RATTLE
Hmm.
This is not good.
Uh . . . spell, spell, spell-a-bob . . .
. . get rid of this big snake mob!
Good job!
POOF

How do we get them OUT of here?
Do NOT make them mad.
They might zap us into frogs!
I like them.
The family tries to be nice.
Time for cake!
Oh, boy! Cake!
The earth is shaking!
Earthquake!
Run!
What is THAT!
Oh! It is just Frank.

Hi, Frank! You are just in time for cake.
AAAHH!
He is cute!
The family has had enough!
Where are you going?
We, uh, need to get more napkins.
Go! Go! Go!
Bye!
Do you think they liked us?
Oh, yes, they LOVED us!

A HOWLING SLUMBER PARTY

In class that day . . .
You cannot leave any of the girls out.
But . . .
That is better, Kim.
Thanks.
You are NOT Invited
Oh, no! Not Spooky Sara!
Later, Wolfy howls with sadness.
He has never spent the night without you.
But only GIRLS are invited.
Sara leaves for the party.
Poor Wolfy! We have to help him!

Wolfy needs a disguise.
At the party:
DING-
DONG!
Who could be at the door?
Who are you?
This is my friend . . . Wanda.
A cheerleader? Cool!
She is very . . . hairy.

Wanda is a good dancer.
Duh! She is a cheerleader!
Hey, look! It is a full moon.
Uh-oh! Full moons make Wolfy . . . WILD.
It is a . . . uh . . . new cheer!
AAAHHHOOOOOOooooHHHH!
AAAHHHOOOOOOooooHHHH!!
AAAHHHOOOOOOooooHHHH!
AAAHHHOOOOOOooooHHHH!!
Cool cheer!

Wolfy is starting to . . . wolf out!
Sara lures Wolfy away.
Come . . . Wanda.
WHOOOOOSH!

AAAHHHOOOoooOHHHH!
AAAHHHOOOoooOHHHH!!
Uh . . . Wanda really gets into her cheers.
Later that night . . .
Surprise!
Shhh! This is not a surprise party!
Meg gets a surprise, too.
TOOOOOOOOOOT!
Aaaahhh!
There is a skeleton in the closet!
I want cake.
Shhh!

But he was right here! Really!
Go home!
But I want cake!
Back at the party, Meg gets ANOTHER surprise.
Want a drink?
Aaaahhh!
But there WAS a ghost in here! Really!
Meg is losing it!

Sara sends Ghosty home.
!!!
Who wants cake?
There is a ghost AND a skeleton out there!
Not again, Meg.
Wow, look at the time! I should get going.
Sara packs her bag.
Why are you leaving?
Um, I forgot to . . . wash my cat. Thanks for inviting me.
So . . . do you think they liked you?
Who cares? I already have the BEST friends in the world!